P9-CJS-479

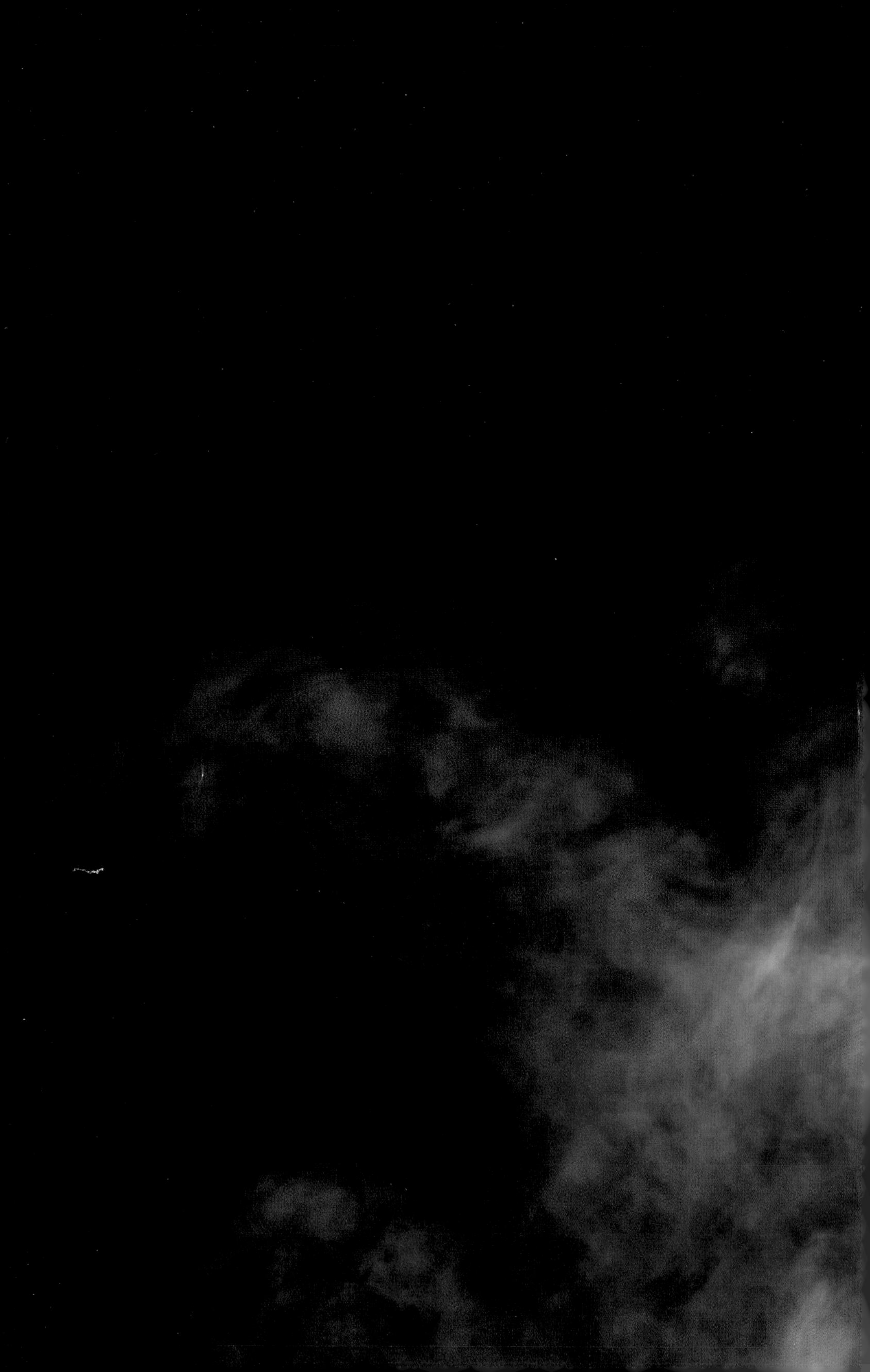

SIMON SPOTLIGHT
An imprint of Simon & Schuster Children's Publishing Division
1230 Avenue of the Americas, New York, New York 10020
This Simon Spotlight edition May 2023

For information about special discounts for bulk purchases, please contact Simon & Schuster Special Sales at 1-866-506-1949 or business@simonandschuster.com. Designed by Nicholas Sciacca. Text by Matthew J. Gilbert. Based on the text by Michael Teitelbaum. Art Services by Glass House Graphics. Art by Giusi Lo Piccolo. Lettering by Giuseppe Naselli/Grafimated Cartoon. Supervision by Salvatore Di Marco/Grafimated Cartoon. The illustrations for this book were rendered digitally. Manufactured in China 0223 SCP
10 9 8 7 6 5 4 3 2
This book has been cataloged by the Library of Congress.
ISBN 978-1-6659-3152-6 (hc)
ISBN 978-1-6659-3151-9 (pbk)
ISBN 978-1-6659-3153-3 (ebook)

# THE SHOW MUST GO ON!

WRITTEN BY P. J. NIGHT
ILLUSTRATED BY
GIUSI LO PICCOLO
AT GLASS HOUSE GRAPHICS

SIMON SPOTLIGHT
NEW YORK LONDON TORONTO SNEY NEW DELHI

PROLOGUE
THIRTY YEARS AGO...
MS. WORMHOUSE...
THE LAST SLEEPOVER
...YOU'RE FIRED.
AND WE'RE CANCELLING YOUR PLAY. IT IS HEREBY BANNED FOREVER.
BANNED?
JUST BE GRATEFUL YOU'RE NOT IN HANDCUFFS.

FIRE ME IF YOU WISH. BUT THIS PLAY WILL BE PERFORMED.
MAYBE. BUT NOT HERE AT THOMAS JEFFERSON MIDDLE SCHOOL.
NOT EVER.
I'M SEEING TO IT THAT ALL COPIES OF THE PLAY ARE DESTROYED.
THE LAST SLEEPOVER
SWIPE
A GIRL DIED LAST NIGHT. ON THIS SCHOOL'S STAGE. IN YOUR PLAY.
DOESN'T THAT MEAN ANYTHING TO YOU?
DON'T YOU SEE...? STRANGE THINGS HAVE BEEN HAPPENING AT THIS SCHOOL SINCE THE DAY YOU ARRIVED.
IT'S ALMOST LIKE YOUR PLAY IS...CURSED.

BAH!
YOU SHOULDN'T LET YOUR FEARS GET THE BEST OF YOU.
TOO LATE.
GOOD RIDDANCE!
THE LAST

T EVER SHOW
YOUR FACE
HERE AGAIN!
THERE SHE IS!
HOW DARE YOU!
YOU OUGHT TO BE IN JAIL!

THIS IS YOUR FAULT!
YOUR PLAY!
THE SHOW MUST GO ON, MILDRED.
DON'T EVER SHOW YOUR FACE HERE AGAIN!
YOU CAN FIRE ME...BUT YOU CANNOT STOP MY PLAY!
THE SHOW MUST GO ON.
THE SHOW WILL GO ON!

PRESENT DAY
THOMAS JEFFERSON MIDDLE
YOU KNOW, YOU NEED, UNIQUE, NEW YORK...
DO RE MI FA SOL LA TI DO...!
BREE, YOU TRYING TO WEAR A HOLE IN THE CARPET?
LIS! AHHH! SO GLAD YOU CAME.
OF COURSE! YOU THINK YOU'RE THE ONLY ONE WHO WANTS TO BE IN THE PLAY?

I'VE DREAMED ABOUT ACTING FOR AS LONG AS I CAN REMEMBER.
I'VE JUST NEVER HAD THE GUTS TO AUDITION FOR ANYTHING.
I FEEL LIKE I'VE JUST BEEN WAITING FOR MY MOMENT.
ANXIOUS TO BEGIN YOUR NEW LIFE IN THE THEATER?
SPEAKING OF WAITING...WHERE IS MR. GOMEZ? WEREN'T WE SUPPOSED TO START, LIKE, TEN MINUTES AGO?
SOMETHING LIKE THAT-
CLUNK!

WHO IS THAT?
WHAT'S GOING ON?
WAIT... WHAT HAPPENED TO MR. GOMEZ?
I DON'T KNOW...

LADIES AND GENTLEMEN, MAY I HAVE YOUR ATTENTION PLEASE?
MY NAME IS MS. HOLLOWS.
UNFORTUNATELY, MR. GOMEZ HAD AN ACCIDENT YESTERDAY AFTERNOON.
SO HE'S NOT PHYSICALLY ABLE TO BE INVOLVED IN THIS YEAR'S PRODUCTION.

GAAAAHHHH!
CREEEEAAAK
I'M TOLD HE BROKE HIS LEG.
THWAAAAM!

HENCE I'LL BE TAKING HIS PLACE...
AS YOUR SUBSTITUTE DRAMA TEACHER...
...AND YOUR DIRECTOR FOR THIS YEAR'S PLAY.
PASS THESE AROUND.
I WAS REALLY LOOKING FORWARD TO WORKING WITH MR. GOMEZ.
ME TOO! I HOPE HE'S OKAY.
UGHHHH... NNNN...
THE SCRIPT I HAVE SELECTED FOR US TO PERFORM IS CALLED...
THE LAST SLEEPOVER

...THE LAST SLEEPOVER.
THE LAST SLEEEPOVER
by
M.P.
Wormhouse
OOOOH! SOUNDS CREEPY. I LIKE IT!

YOU ARE TO READ THE PLAY THIS WEEKEND AND DECIDE WHICH ROLE YOU'LL BE AUDITIONING FOR.
AUDITIONS WILL BE HELD AFTER SCHOOL ON MONDAY. I WILL SEE YOU THEN.

YOU ALL RIGHT, GABRIELLE?
OH... YES, SORRY, MS. HOLLOWS.
I WAS JUST...UH... DAYDREAMING.
MOMENTS LATER...
THAT WAS WEIRD.
WHAT WAS WEIRD?

MS. HOLLOWS KNEW MY NAME AND WE'VE NEVER MET.
AND NOT JUST MY NICKNAME. MY REAL NAME.
AUDITO
NO ONE EVER GUESSES "BREE" IS SHORT FOR "GABRIELLE."
SHE HAS A ROLL CALL SHEET. THAT'S PROBABLY HOW SHE KNEW. I BET SHE WILL CALL ME MELISSA, EVEN THOUGH EVERYONE CALLS ME "LIS."
HONK!
THAT'S MY MOM. I GOTTA GO. BYE! DON'T GET TOO SCARED READING THE PLAY!
'KAY, I WON'T. SEE YA!

DON'T GET TOO SCARED...
THE LAST SLEEPOVER...BY M.P. WORMHOUSE.
AUDITORIUM

# CHAPTER 2

YEARS AGO, A GIRL NAMED MILLIE LIVED IN THIS HOUSE.
SHE WAS A SHY GIRL WHO KEPT TO HERSELF MOST OF THE TIME.
YOU'RE MY CLOSEST FRIENDS.

I'VE JUST HAD A WONDERFUL IDEA! LET'S STAY UP ALL NIGHT AND TELL GHOST STORIES AND HAVE PILLOW FIGHTS.

THE THING SHE WANTED MOST IN THE WORLD WAS TO BE INVITED TO A SLEEPOVER.

AND AS FATE WOULD HAVE IT, A CLASSMATE NAMED GABBY WAS ABOUT TO HOST ONE.
SHE INVITED EVERY GIRL IN HER CLASS ...
...EXCEPT MILLIE.
SORRY, THERE'S JUST NO MORE ROOM. IF I INVITE YOU, THEN I HAVE TO INVITE ALL EIGHT OF YOUR STUFFED ANIMALS...
...SINCE THEY'RE THE ONLY FRIENDS YOU HAVE.

MILLIE WAS CRUSHED...BUT THE WORST WAS STILL TO COME.
GABBY HAD MANY, MANY SLEEPOVERS...
...SOMETIMES FOUR OR MORE A YEAR...
...AND SHE NEVER INVITED MILLIE TO A SINGLE ONE.
SOON AFTER, MILLIE GOT SICK.
VERY SICK.
SHE DIED... NEVER HAVING GOTTEN HER WISH TO ATTEND A SLEEPOVER.

MILLIE'S FAMILY MOVED AWAY SHORTLY AFTER AND SOLD THE HOUSE...
...TO A FAMILY WITH A LITTLE GIRL...
...WHO WAS ALREADY DREAMING OF HAVING SLEEPOVERS OF HER OWN.
AND THAT'S WHEN THE HAUNTING BEGAN.

Every girl who had a sleepover in this house experienced strange things.

It is said *that* Millie's ghost haunts this place...

...and will keep haunting it...
...until she attends a sleepover.

...until she attends a sleepover.
LIGHTS GO OUT ALL OF A SUDDEN.
GIRLS SCREAM WITH FEAR.
"LIGHTS GO OUT ALL OF A SUDDEN. GIRLS SCREAM WITH FEAR."
Juliet
THIS PLAY IS SO SCARY.
GASP!
WHATCHA GOT THERE...?
JEEZ. JUMPY MUCH?
IT'S A COPY OF THE PLAY WE'RE PUTTING ON THIS YEAR.

YOU'RE AUDITIONING?! MY FLY-ON-THE-WALL SISTER WANTS TO STEP INTO THE SPOTLIGHT?
YOU'RE SUCH A DRAMA QUEEN.
I'M TEASING! WHAT'S THE PLAY ABOUT?
IT'S ABOUT A HAUNTING. IT'S REALLY CREEPY.
IN FACT, IT'S BEEN GIVING ME A WEIRD FEELING READING IT. LIKE IT'S GETTING UNDER MY SKIN.
YOU KNOW WHAT I THINK? THAT'S JUST NERVES.
YOU'RE NOT CUT OUT FOR THE STAGE.
WHY DON'T YOU MAKE YOUR EXIT, STAGE RIGHT?
WHATEVER.

AND THANKS AS ALWAYS FOR YOUR SISTERLY ADVICE!
HAPPY TO HELP!
UGH!
YOU KNOW WHAT I THINK? I THINK MEGAN DOESN'T WANT TO SHARE THE SPOTLIGHT WITH ANYONE. ESPECIALLY ME.
WELL, GUESS WHAT?
I AM AUDITIONING, AND I WILL GET THE LEAD!
FLIP
I'LL SHOW HER.

12:19
AM
12:19
AM

12:31 AM
AS BREE DRIFTED OFF TO SLEEP...
...SHE COULDN'T SHAKE THE HAUNTING PRESENCE OF THE PLAY AND ITS CHARACTERS.
SHE SPENT THE NIGHT TOSSING AND TURNING...
2:01 AM
...HER DREAMS BLENDING WITH WAKING THOUGHTS.
IT WAS THE FIRST OF MANY RESTLESS NIGHTS.

5:32
AM

# CHAPTER 3

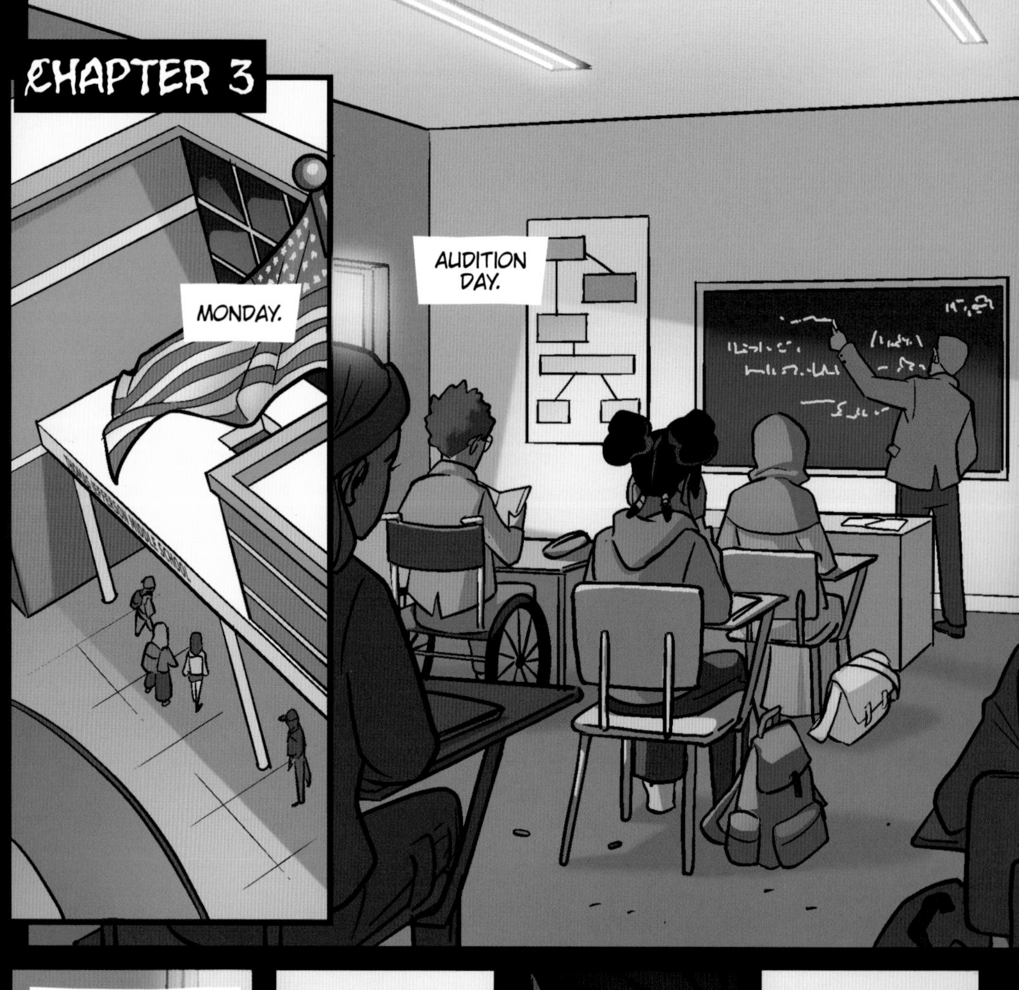
MONDAY.
AUDITION DAY.

BREE WAS FOCUSED ON ONE THING AND ONE THING ONLY...

...HER BIG CHANCE.

RIIIIIIIIII

-WHUNG!
BREE!

SAVED YOU A SEAT!

WHAT'D YOU THINK OF THE SCRIPT? WASN'T IT SCARY?!

IT TOTALLY CREEPED ME OUT. BUT I COULDN'T PUT IT DOWN.
IT WAS LIKE SOMETHING WAS *FORCING ME* TO KEEP READING.
MATH

SO TRUE! WELL...I DECIDED...
I'M READING FOR THE PART OF RACHEL, CARRIE'S BEST FRIEND.
AWESOME! I'M GOING FOR CARRIE!
HOW COOL WOULD IT BE IF WE GOT TO PLAY BEST FRIENDS IN THE PLAY?
WELL, THAT'S ***NEVER*** GOING TO HAPPEN.
AND WHY IS THAT?
BECAUSE I'LL BE PLAYING CARRIE. THIS AUDITION IS MERELY A FORMALITY.

JUST BECAUSE YOU'VE GOTTEN THE LEAD IN OTHER PLAYS DOESN'T MEAN YOU'LL BE THE LEAD IN THIS ONE.
WELL, LOOK WHO DECIDED TO SPEAK UP. LITTLE MISS WALLFLOWER.
NEVER DANCES AT A PARTY. NEVER SAYS TWO WORDS.
YOU'RE MORE SUITED TO PLAY THE GHOST.
CREEEEAAAAAK

LADIES AND GENTLEMEN...
...I TRUST YOU ALL ENJOYED THE SCRIPT.
HOPEFULLY, YOU WEREN'T TOO SCARED.

LET US BEGIN. WILL THOSE AUDITIONING FOR THE ROLE OF CARRIE PLEASE LINE UP TO MY RIGHT, HERE ON THE STAGE.

QUICKLY NOW.
BUMP
IGNORE HER, BREE THOUGHT.
THIS IS IT. NO TURNING BACK NOW.
AUDITIONS

AND THAT'S WHEN THE HAUNTING BEGAN–
OPEN CASTING
NEXT!
CHLOE
TIFFANY
BREE
EMILY
KELLY

I HEARD THE WHOLE STORY... FROM THE OLD WOMAN...WHO LIVES NEXT DOOR-
UGH. NEXT!
BRIAN
AND... NEXT!

OPEN CASTING CALL
TODAY
WHICH SCENE HAVE YOU CHOSEN, GABRIELLE?
GULP
I'M GOING TO DO CARRIE'S MONOLOGUE DURING THE FLOATING OBJECTS SCENE.
VERY WELL. BEGIN.
BREE HAD THOUGHT ABOUT WHO THE CHARACTER OF CARRIE WAS. SHE DIDN'T WANT TO JUST READ HER LINES.
SHE WANTED TO *BECOME* CARRIE.

I TOLD YOU, THIS HOUSE IS HAUNTED BY THE GIRL WHO DIED BEFORE SHE EVER GOT INVITED TO A SLEEPOVER. HER NAME WAS MILLIE.
I FEEL KINDA SORRY FOR HER, BUT SHE IS A GHOST. AND WHO WANTS A GHOST AT THEIR SLEEPOVER?
I KNOW HOW IT SOUNDS, BUT SHE'S CONNECTED TO THIS HOUSE. WELL, IT'S MY HOUSE NOW, NOT HERS...
AND SHE'S NOT INVITED. END OF STORY.

AND... SCENE.

THANK YOU FOR THAT, ***GABRIELLE***.

YOU MAY TAKE YOUR SEAT.

AND FINALLY, TIFFANY.

AUDITIONS
OPEN CASTING CALL
TODAY

CAN I TRY THIS WITH AN ACCENT?

OOF UGH

GIRL. GIRL. GIRL!
YOU WERE AMAZING!
REALLY? I WAS?
MATH
TIFFANY DOESN'T STAND A CHANCE.
...IT'S MY HOUSE NOW, NOT HERS...
SHE'S JUST...NOT... IN-VIIIII-TED!
WHAT IS THIS VOICE SHE'S DOING?
I HAVE NO IDEA.

MANY MONOLOGUES LATER, AFTER THE FINAL AUDITION OF THE DAY...
OPEN CASTING CALL
TODAY

THANK YOU ALL. WHEN I'VE MADE MY DECISION, I WILL POST THE CAST LIST ON THE BULLETIN BOARD.

*GABRIELLE...?*

A WORD?

I'LL TALK TO YOU LATER. MY MOM'S OUTSIDE. TEXT ME!
OKAY!

GABRIELLE...
YES, MS. HOLLOWS?
THIS PLAY HAS BEEN WAITING FOR YOU.
WHAT...?
BUT MS. HOLLOWS DIDN'T ANSWER BREE.
WHAT DOES THAT MEAN?

# CHAPTER 4

CAST LIST
THE NEXT DAY...

IT WAS A STRUGGLE TO PAY ATTENTION IN CLASS.

ALL ANYONE WANTED TO KNOW WAS...WHO MADE THE LIST.

YOU GOT IT! YOU GOT IT!

CAST LIST

Carrie: Gabrielle Hart
Rachel: Melissa Hwang
Laura: Dara Khan
Ghost: Tiffany O'Brian

WOW...

I...
I...I CAN'T BELIEVE IT.
IF YOU THINK *YOU* CAN'T BELIEVE IT, WAIT UNTIL TIFFANY FINDS OUT.
FINDS OUT WHAT...?
EXCUSE ME, TALENT COMING THROUGH!
CAST LIST
CAST LIST
THIS IS SO WRONG! ***THIS IS ALL WRONG!***

WHAT'S WRONG ABOUT IT? YOU AUDITIONED, SHE AUDITIONED.
SHE GOT THE PART.
BUT I AM SUCH A BETTER ACTOR! I HAVE TO BE IN THIS PLAY.
YOU *ARE* IN THE PLAY.
YOU PLAY THE GIRL WHO HAUNTS THE SLEEPOVER.
LOOKS LIKE *YOU'RE* MORE SUITED TO PLAY THE GHOST. HA!
CAST LIST
Gabrielle Hart
Melissa Hwang
Dara Marinelli
Ghost: Tiffany O'Brian
SEE YOU AT REHEARSALS, TIFF!
LIS, DON'T! THE MORE YOU UPSET HER, THE MORE SHE'LL TAKE IT OUT ON ME.
WHAT? YOU WON THAT ROLE FAIR AND SQUARE.

CAST LIST
Carrie: Gabrielle Hart
Rachel: Melissa Hwang
Laura: Dara Marinelli
Ghost: Tiffany O'Brian
I WONDER...
dear you,
YES
YOU
You are amazing!
THIS PLAY...
...HAS BEEN WAITING... *FOR YOU*.

YOU WONDER WHAT?
NOTHING. I'M JUST...TALKING TO MYSELF. THIS IS A LOT.
I'VE GOTTA GET BACK TO CLASS. SEE YOU AT REHEARSAL.
SEE YOU AT REHEARSAL... CARRIE!
BREE SHOULD HAVE BEEN THRILLED TO BE ON THAT LIST.
BUT SOMETHING ABOUT IT FELT OFF.

LATER, AS SHE ARRIVED AT THE VERY FIRST REHEARSAL, BREE FELT AS IF SHE'D STEPPED INTO ANOTHER WORLD.

THE CREW WAS ALREADY TRANSFORMING THE STAGE INTO CARRIE'S BEDROOM. **HER** BEDROOM.

BOO!
AAAAAAHHHH!
YOU CAN'T JUST SNEAK UP ON A PERSON IN THEIR OWN HAUNTED HOUSE. DON'T YOU KNOW THAT?
I DIDN'T KNOW THAT. BUT I'LL TELL YOU WHAT I DO KNOW.
TIFFANY IS *STILL* SULKING.
QUIET ON STAGE!

LADIES AND GENTLEMEN...
...I THANK YOU ALL AGAIN FOR VOLUNTEERING TO BE PART OF THIS PLAY.
NOW, MAY I HAVE ALL OF MY ACTORS ON STAGE PLEASE?
ALLOW ME TO BE THE FIRST TO TELL YOU...
...BREAK A LEG.
FROM THE TOP. SCENE ONE. CARRIE, RACHEL, AND LAURA.
PLACES, PLEASE.

NICE, CARRIE. THIS PLACE LOOKS LIKE IT WAS DECORATED WITH A WRECKING BALL.

MY FAMILY HASN'T HAD THE CHANCE TO FIX UP THE HOUSE YET. BUT I JUST COULDN'T WAIT TO HAVE MY FIRST SLEEPOVER.
IT HELPS MAKE THE PLACE FEEL LIKE HOME.
YEAH, IF YOUR HOME'S BEEN CONDEMNED!
RUMBLE
ZAAAAAP!

GAAAAHHHH!
LAURA?
SORRY. I'M JUST A LITTLE AFRAID OF THUNDER.
ZZZRRT!
ZZZRRRP!
OKAY, NOW I'M OFFICIALLY CREEPED OUT.
IS THAT SUPPOSED TO BE DOING... *THAT*?
HOLD THE LIGHTS! TAKE FIVE, EVERYONE. VERY GOOD START.

AS MS. HOLLOWS GAVE HER NOTES, THE LIGHTS FLICKERED UNCONTROLLABLY... ON THEIR OWN.
BZZ
BZZZZZ
BZZ!
THAT'S ENOUGH CHANDELIER EFFECTS NOW, TECH CREW. PLEASE LEAVE ALL THE LIGHTS ON.
ZZZ
FLASH
ZZ
FLASH
WHAT'S GOING ON?
SOMEONE HIT A BUTTON!
WHAT BUTTON?!
FLASH-ZZ-FLASH
ZZ-FLASH
LOOK OUT!
POP-HISSS

WE'RE NOT DOING THIS, MS. HOLLOWS! WE'RE NOT TOUCHING THE LIGHTS!
OUR LIGHTING BOARD ISN'T EVEN HOOKED UP YET, MS. HOLLOWS.
CAN WE DO SOMETHING BEFORE WE BLOW A FUSE HERE!?
ZZZZRRRRRRRR!
AND THEN, IN A FLASH...

...EVERYTHING WENT DARK.

# CHAPTER 5

FLASHLIGHTS!
I'M GOING TO SEE IF I CAN FIND OUT WHAT'S GOING ON WITH THE LIGHTS. EVERYONE, STAY PUT!
GREAT, NOW WHAT DO WE DO?
I HAVE AN IDEA. WHY DON'T WE SIT IN A CIRCLE AND PRETEND THIS IS A REAL SLEEPOVER?
AND YOU KNOW WHAT EVERY SLEEPOVER NEEDS...
...A GHOST STORY!

UNLESS OF COURSE...YOU CAN'T HANDLE IT, WALLFLOWER?
I'M FINE. IT CAN ONLY HELP US GET INTO CHARACTER.

OKAY, WHO'S GOT A GOOD GHOST STORY?

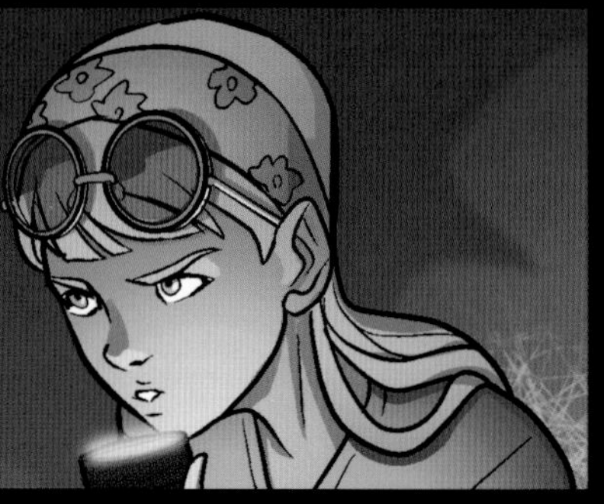
I DO. IT'S ABOUT THIS VERY PLAY WE'RE PERFORMING.
I DID A LITTLE RESEARCH BEFORE AUDITIONS.

THAT'S WHAT REAL ACTORS DO.
THIS PLAY WAS ACTUALLY PERFORMED THIRTY YEARS AGO. AT THIS SCHOOL. IN THIS AUDITORIUM.
ON THIS EXACT STAGE.

A CREEPY TEACHER NAMED WORMHOUSE WROTE THE PLAY AND DEMANDED THE SCHOOL PUT IT ON.
FROM DAY ONE, THE REHEARSALS WERE PLAGUED BY *STRANGE* INCIDENTS...
TJ

PROPS MYSTERIOUSLY BREAKING IN THE MIDDLE OF A SCENE...
...LIGHTS GOING ON AND OFF...MAKING IT IMPOSSIBLE TO KEEP THE ACTORS OR THE CREW TRULY SAFE.
...SCENERY COLLAPSING FOR NO REASON...
KINDA LIKE WHAT'S HAPPENING RIGHT NOW.
SOMEHOW, THEY MADE IT TO OPENING NIGHT.
TJ Soccer

AND AS SOON AS THE GIRL PLAYING CARRIE STEPPED OUT ONTO THE STAGE...
SNAP!
...SOMETHING FELL FROM THE RAFTERS-
YIEEEEE!!
IT STRUCK AND KILLED HER INSTANTLY.
AAAAH!

GASP!
BACK THEN, THERE WERE RUMORS THAT THE PLAY ITSELF WAS CURSED...
...AND THAT WHOEVER PLAYS THE LEAD...IS DESTINED TO *DIE*!!!
CLICK!
RIGHT ON CUE, JUST AS TIFFANY SAID THE WORD "DIE," THE LIGHTS BLAZED BACK TO LIFE.

THE ONLY THING WORSE THAN HAVING EVERYONE STARE AT HER WAS THE THOUGHT THAT CREPT INTO BREE'S HEAD.
COULD THE PLAY REALLY BE CURSED...? AM I...DOOMED?
THANK YOU, TIFFANY, FOR THAT... INTERESTING BIT OF FOLKLORE.
GOOD NEWS: OUR LIGHTS HAVE BEEN FIXED.
BAD NEWS: WE ARE OUT OF TIME FOR TODAY.
ARE YOU OKAY...?
COME BACK REFRESHED AND READY FOR A FULL REHEARSAL TOMORROW.
THE SHOW MUST GO ON!

A RAGING THUNDERSTORM AWAITED THE KIDS AFTER REHEARSAL.
THIS EXPLAINS WHY THE LIGHTS WENT OUT.
FOR SURE. AND HEY, DON'T LISTEN TO TIFFANY AND HER MADE-UP GHOST STORIES. SHE'S JUST TRYING TO GET INTO YOUR HEAD.
DRIP
DRIP
DRIP
DRIP
DRIP
I SEE MY MOM'S CAR. TEXT YOU LATER!
BYE!
GABRIELLE...?
OH, IT'S YOU.

I HAVE SOMETHING TO TELL YOU... I THINK YOU'RE GOING TO HATE PLAYING THE LEAD.
IN FACT, I BET YOU'LL BE SORRY YOU EVER TRIED OUT FOR THIS PLAY.
WHAT'S THAT SUPPOSED TO MEAN?
IT'S A LOT OF PRESSURE. ALL THOSE LINES. EVERYTHING REVOLVING AROUND YOU.
EVERYONE ***STARING*** AT YOU.
IT'S BECAUSE THEY'RE DEPENDING ON YOU. ONE LITTLE MISTAKE AND YOU COULD RUIN THE WHOLE PLAY.
I'D QUIT NOW IF I WERE YOU.
BUT THANKFULLY... I'M NOT YOU.

CRAAARRRRRRACK!
AUDITORIUM
BREE STOOD THERE IN THE RAIN AS A STORM OF EMOTIONS BREWED INSIDE HER.
WAS THAT A THREAT?
LATER THAT SAME RAINY NIGHT...

...AFTER HOURS OF HOMEWORK, BREE FELT HERSELF DRIFTING IN AND OUT OF SLEEP.

HOW DID I GET HERE?!

IS THIS... THE LAST SLEEPOVER?
WHAT AM I DOING SITTING IN THE AUDIENCE?
WHAT'S GOING ON?
AT THAT MOMENT, A CROWD OF PEOPLE SUDDENLY APPEARED OUT OF THIN AIR, FILLING THE AUDITORIUM.
SHE HAD NEVER SEEN THE PLACE SO PACKED.
WHAT ARE THEY WEARING? BREE WONDERED. WHAT YEAR IS THIS?

NONE OF THIS MAKES ANY SENSE. IS SCHOOL HAVING A '90S NIGHT OR SOMETHING?
CLAP!
CLAP!
CLAP!
NICE, CARRIE. THE PLACE LOOKS LIKE IT WAS DECORATED WITH A WRECKING BALL.
HAHAHAHAHA
MY FAMILY HASN'T HAD THE CHANCE TO FIX UP THE HOUSE YET.
BUT I JUST COULDN'T WAIT TO HAVE MY FIRST SLEEPOVER.
THIS IS THE SCENE WE REHEARSED TODAY. OKAY, NOW THIS IS OFFICIALLY WEIRD.

THERE WAS NO TIME TO FIGURE OUT WHAT WAS HAPPENING. A SHARP SNAPPING SOUND CAUGHT BREE'S ATTENTION-
SNAP!
PANIC FLOODED THROUGH HER AS SHE SAW THE CHANDELIER COME LOOSE...
...PLUNGING STRAIGHT DOWN AT THE GIRL PLAYING CARRIE.

YIEEEEEEE!!!
LOOK OUT!

# CHAPTER 6

HUFF
PUFF
HUFF
PUFF
BREE'S HEART WAS POUNDING. HER HANDS WERE SHAKING.
SIGH
IT WAS ALL A TERRIBLE DREAM.
KNOCK
KNOCK
YOU OKAY? I HEARD SCREAMING.
I...JUST NEED...A MINUTE.

A FEW MINUTES LATER...
MORNING. YOU LOOK HORRIBLE.
GEE, THANKS. I DIDN'T SLEEP WELL.
BAD DREAMS?
YEP.

CHEW CHEW-
ABOUT THE SHOW?

YEP.
SOUNDS LIKE STAGE FRIGHT.

NO, I'M FINE WHEN I'M ONSTAGE. IT'S HARD TO EXPLAIN, BUT...
THE PLAY IS GIVING ME THE CREEPS.
CRUNCH
IT'S A SCARY PLAY, BREE. GIVING PEOPLE THE CREEPS IS WHAT IT'S SUPPOSED TO DO.
YEAH, BUT IT'S SUPPOSED TO GIVE THE AUDIENCE THE CREEPS...
...NOT THE ACTORS!
PLUNK!
I TOLD YOU, SOME PEOPLE AREN'T CUT OUT FOR THE THEATER...
...THERE'S NO SHAME IN THAT.
SHOVE

THANKS FOR BEING SO SYMPATHETIC! YOU'RE SUCH A GOOD SISTER!
BREE!
SLAM
THAT'S THE LAST TIME I GO TO MEGAN WITH MY PROBLEMS, BREE THOUGHT.
EVERYTHING IS FINE. IT WAS JUST A DREAM. THAT'S ALL.
A DREAM.
BUS

AFTER A DAY OF CLASSES, REHEARSALS COULD FINALLY BEGIN AGAIN.
THE LIGHTS WERE UP AND THE STAGE WAS SET...FOR A TRULY HAUNTING SCENE.

LOOK, THEY ADDED SLEEPING BAGS! AND LANTERNS! IT LOOKS LIKE A REAL SLEEPOVER.
LADIES AND GENTLEMEN...

...LISTEN UP! IT'S TIME TO "DO THE WORK," AS THEY SAY IN THE THEATER.

LET'S RUN THE CARRIE AND RACHEL SCENE, PLEASE. FROM THE TOP!

CARRIE... YOU'RE SUPPOSED TO BE UPSET IN THIS SCENE. SO REALLY SELL IT. I WANT TO SEE YOU PACING. ANXIOUS.

ACTION!
IT HAPPENED AGAIN.
ONLY NOW IT'S HAPPENING EVERYWHERE.
WHAT DO YOU MEAN, EVERYWHERE?
WHEN I WALK DOWN THE HALLWAYS...
WHEN I WALK HOME FROM SCHOOL...
EVEN WHEN I GO FROM ONE ROOM IN MY HOUSE TO ANOTHER...
...I FEEL IT.

HAVE YOU ACTUALLY SEEN ANYONE?
AND WHAT'S WORSE-
THERE'S A WORSE PART?
I HEAR FOOTSTEPS ALL THE TIME. AND WHEN I TURN AROUND, NO ONE IS THERE!

THOUGH IT WASN'T IN THE SCRIPT, BREE SUDDENLY FELT COMPELLED TO MOVE TO THE FRONT OF THE STAGE.
I'M POSITIVE THAT WHOEVER IS FOLLOWING ME...

...MEANS TO DO ME HARM!
JUST THEN, BREE HEARD A STRANGE SOUND FROM ABOVE.
SNAP!
ADRENALINE SHOT THROUGH BREE'S BODY, BUT SHE COULDN'T MOVE. SHE WAS FROZEN WITH FEAR...

...WATCHING HER WORST NIGHTMARES COME TRUE!
GAAAAA—!
AAAAA—!
AAAAAHHHHH!

SMAAAASH!
BREE!
HELP HER!
CAREFUL!

HOW DID THIS HAPPEN?
SOMEONE CALL JANITORIAL ABOUT THIS GLASS. AND CALL THE SCHOOL NURSE!
I'M FINE, REALLY.
WHAT HAPPENED? I HEARD A LOUD–
BREE STARED AT TIFFANY AND WONDERED WHERE SHE HAD BEEN THIS WHOLE TIME.
*WHAT AM I THINKING...? TIFFANY WOULDN'T TRY TO HURT ME... WOULD SHE?*

IT WAS JUST AN ACCIDENT. I'M FINE, EVERYONE.
CAN WE TRY THE SCENE AGAIN? THIS TIME, WITHOUT THE FALLING LIGHT.

HAHAHAHAHA

BRAVO, **GABRIELLE**. A TRUE PROFESSIONAL. SO BRAVE.
CLAP!
CLAP!
CLAP!

YES, SO BRAVE. GO, BREE.
CLAP!
CLAP!
CLAP!

CLAP!
CLAP!
CLAP!
NOT EVEN OPENING NIGHT, AND ALREADY A STANDING OVATION!

LATER, WHEN REHEARSAL ENDED, BREE DECIDED IT WAS TIME TO TELL MELISSA ABOUT ALL THE DRAMA SHE WAS HAVING... OFFSTAGE!
AUDITORIUM
TODAY WAS A NIGHTMARE. BUT IT WAS NOTHING COMPARED TO THE DREAM I HAD LAST NIGHT.
I DREAMED I WAS SITTING IN THE AUDIENCE OF THAT AUDITORIUM, WATCHING A PLAY ON OPENING NIGHT.
IT WAS THE LAST SLEEPOVER!
SO YOU WERE DREAMING ABOUT US DOING THE SHOW?
THAT'S JUST IT, LIS. IT WASN'T US.
THE PEOPLE IN MY DREAM WERE WEARING OLD CLOTHES, LIKE THEY WERE FROM THE 1990S OR SOMETHING—THE AUDIENCE AND THE ACTORS!
I THINK I WAS WATCHING THE ORIGINAL PERFORMANCE. THE ONE TIFFANY WAS TELLING US ABOUT!

JUST BECAUSE OF THEIR CLOTHES? RETRO IS IN RIGHT NOW.
NOT JUST THE CLOTHES.
THE ACCIDENT TIFFANY DESCRIBED... I WATCHED IT FROM THE AUDIENCE. I SAW THE LIGHT FALL ON THE ACTRESS PLAYING CARRIE WITH MY OWN EYES.
YIEEEEE!!
IT WAS SO MUCH LIKE WHAT ALMOST HAPPENED TO ME JUST NOW!
SO WHAT... SOME EVIL SPIRIT IS CONNECTED TO THE PLAY? A REAL ***LITTLE GHOST GIRL***?
HELLO! TIFFANY MADE THAT STUFF UP TO GET TO YOU.

IF A GIRL REALLY DIED AT OUR SCHOOL, ON THIS STAGE...
...EVERYONE WOULD KNOW ABOUT IT, RIGHT?
YOU'RE RIGHT. THERE WOULD BE A RECORD OF IT.

EXACTLY. NOW, C'MON, MY MOM CAN GIVE YOU A RIDE HOME.
NO, THAT'S OKAY...
DITORIUM
...I HAVE SOMEWHERE I HAVE TO GO FIRST.

MAYBE MELISSA WAS RIGHT. BUT BREE HAD TO BE SURE.
THOMAS JEFFERSON MIDDLE SCHOOL LIBRARY
SO SHE WENT TO THE ONE PLACE WITH ALL THE ANSWERS.
SHE WOULD GET TO THE BOTTOM OF THIS. AND SHE WOULD DO IT NOW...
...BEFORE ANOTHER REHEARSAL TOOK PLACE.

BREE HART.
HI, MR. HARRIS.
YOU'RE HERE LATE. BIG PROJECT?
I NEED TO LOOK INTO THE HISTORY OF THIS SCHOOL.
AH! ONE OF MY FAVORITE TOPICS...SINCE I'M OLD AS DIRT.
ANYTHING IN PARTICULAR? OR JUST GENERAL TRIVIA?
I WANT TO KNOW THE HISTORY OF THE PLAY WE'RE PERFORMING THIS YEAR.
I BELIEVE IT MAY HAVE BEEN STAGED BEFORE AND FOR ONE NIGHT ONLY.
THAT WAS A BIT BEFORE MY TIME, BELIEVE IT OR NOT. AND NOW THAT YOU MENTION IT, I DO SORT OF RECALL HEARING ABOUT AN INCIDENT.
FOLLOW ME...

THE SCHOOL ARCHIVES!
I HAVE EVERY ISSUE EVER PUBLISHED OF ***THE JEFFERSONIAN***, OUR SCHOOL PAPER. EVEN THE VERY FIRST ISSUE FROM 1971!
1983 1984 1985 1986 1987 1988 1989
I STARTED HERE IN THE YEAR 2000. SO, WHERE DO WE START...'90S? '80S?
THIRTY YEARS AGO. EARLY 1990S. THE PLAY IS CALLED ***THE LAST SLEEPOVER***.
'90, '91, '92... AND '93! JUST AS HEAVY AND DUSTY AS EVER.
1990
1991
PICK YOUR POISON.
I'LL TAKE 1993.
DRAMA... DRAMA... HERE IT IS!

The Jeffersonian
January 1993

# THE JEFFERSONIAN TJ MS

## LAST SLEEPOVER IS A SCHOOL FIRST!

This year's school play is an original called The Last Sleepover, written & directed by drama teacher Mildred P. Wormhouse.

MILDRED? MILLIE IS SHORT FOR MILDRED!
EXCUSE ME?
I'M JUST THINKING OUT LOUD.
"THE PLAY WILL BE HELD IN THE SCHOOL AUDITORIUM ON MARCH 6TH... "
FLIP FLIP FLIP FLIP FLIP
MARCH '93, MARCH '93... GOT IT!
OH MY.
NO. IT CAN'T BE.
THE JEFFERSONIAN
TJ MS
The Jeffersonian
March 1993
TRAGEDY ON STAGE:
LEAD ACTRESS DIES ON OPENING NIGHT!

# CHAPTER 8

Tragedy struck on opening night of the school play when a stage light fell and killed eighth-grader Gabrielle Ashford.
Gabrielle Ashford

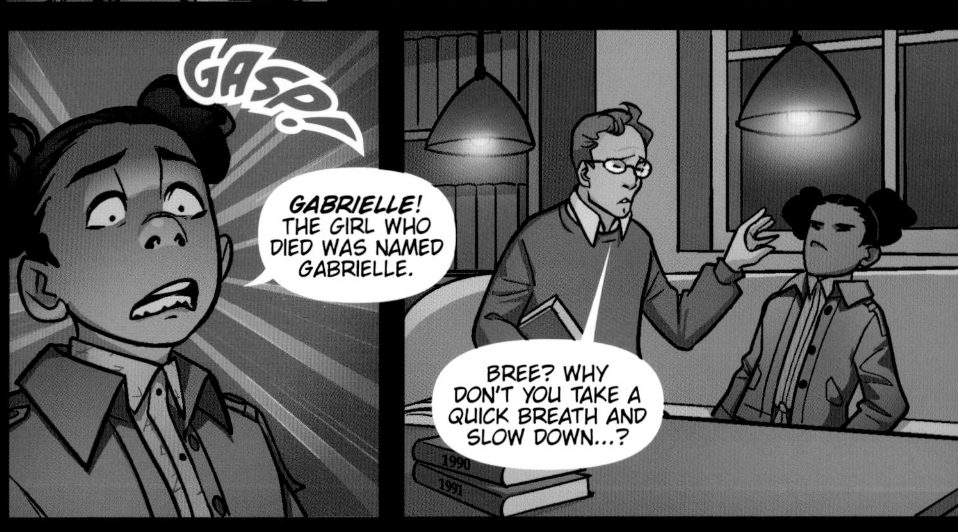
GASP!
GABRIELLE! THE GIRL WHO DIED WAS NAMED GABRIELLE.
BREE? WHY DON'T YOU TAKE A QUICK BREATH AND SLOW DOWN...?
1990
1991

DON'T YOU SEE, MR. HARRIS? IT'S ALL SO FREAKY! THE PLAY HASN'T BEEN PERFORMED SINCE THEN. UNTIL NOW.
AND I'M PLAYING THE LEAD.

AND MY NAME IS "GABRIELLE" TOO!

I DON'T THINK I'VE EVER HEARD ANYONE AT THIS SCHOOL CALL YOU BY YOUR FULL NAME BEFORE.
I APPRECIATE YOUR HELP, MR. HARRIS. I'M HEADING HOME NOW.
NO, THERE'S ONLY ONE PERSON WHO DOES.
AND I'VE GOT TO TALK TO HER.
A MILLION THOUGHTS RACED THROUGH BREE'S MIND AT THAT MOMENT.
MILDRED IS MILLIE THE GHOST. GABRIELLE IS ME! TIFFANY'S STORY WAS TRUE! WHICH MEANS...THE PLAY REALLY IS CURSED!
I'VE GOT TO TALK TO MS. HOLLOWS TOMORROW!

BREE STRODE QUICKLY ACROSS THE SCHOOL'S MAIN LAWN.
BUT AS SHE LISTENED TO THE SOUND OF HER OWN FOOTSTEPS...
THUMP
THUMP
THUMP
...SHE SWORE SHE COULD HEAR A *SECOND SET OF FOOTSTEPS* IN THE GRASS...
THUMP
THUMP

THUMP
THUMP
...MINGLING WITH HER OWN.
AS IF SOMEONE WAS FOLLOWING HER...

...ALL THE WAY HOME.
Out getting groceries with Megan. Back in time for a late dinner. Snacks in the fridge. Love, M & D
GREAT. JUST WHEN I DON'T WANT TO BE AT HOME ALONE...
...I'VE GOT THE PLACE ALL TO MYSELF.

O-KAYYY...
BREE'S HEART STARTED POUNDING.

SHE REACHED FOR HER PHONE. SHE WAS USED TO USING THE FLASHLIGHT ON IT WHENEVER THERE WAS A POWER OUTAGE.
CLICK!
BUT THIS WAS DIFFERENT.

SHE NOTICED THAT ALTHOUGH EVERY LIGHT IN THE HOUSE SEEMED TO BE OUT...
8:08
...THEY HADN'T ACTUALLY LOST POWER. THE CLOCKS WERE STILL ON AND KEEPING CORRECT TIME.

FLIP
FLIP
FLIP
FLIP
WEIRD.
ONLY THE LIGHTS SEEMED TO BE AFFECTED.

DID WE BLOW A FUSE OR SOMETHING...?
8:08 PM
FLIP FLIP

BREE WAS MORE CREEPED OUT THAN EVER.
THIS IS LIKE A SCENE FROM THE PLAY, SHE THOUGHT.
GASP!
AS THE LIGHT PASSED THE WINDOW...

...SHE SPOTTED A FACE STARING AT HER FROM OUTSIDE!

CHAPTER 9
GAAAAHHH!!
THUD
BREE WAS SCARED TO MOVE.
BUT SHE WAS EVEN MORE FRIGHTENED OF STAYING IN THE DARK... WHERE *THAT FACE* WAS HIDING...AND WAITING... AND ***WATCHING***.

BREE YANKED THE WINDOW OPEN, SEARCHING FOR THAT HAUNTING FACE...
CREEEAAAK
...BUT IT HAD VANISHED.

BREE! WE'RE HOME!
MEGAN...

BREE!
HELLO?
MEGAN!
YEAH...?
WERE YOU JUST OUTSIDE MY WINDOW? ARE YOU TRYING TO SCARE ME OUT OF DOING THE PLAY?

WHAT ON EARTH ARE YOU TALKING ABOUT? YOUR SISTER'S BEEN SHOPPING WITH US.
HOW WOULD I EVEN GET UP TO YOUR WINDOW? I CAN'T FLY, YOU KNOW.
WHY ARE YOU HANGING OUT IN THE DARK, KIDDO?
ALL THE LIGHTS WENT OUT AT THE SAME TIME AND–

FLIP
LOOKS LIKE THE LIGHTS WORK JUST FINE.

HONEY, ARE YOU FEELING ALL RIGHT?

NO, SHE'S NOT, MOM. THE PRESSURE OF DOING THIS PLAY IS PROVING TO BE TOO MUCH FOR HER.
MEGAN, GO HELP YOUR FATHER UNLOAD GROCERIES.
FINE.
MOM, I SWEAR, THE LIGHTS WOULDN'T WORK, AND I SAW—

HONEY, CALM DOWN. YOU LOOK LIKE YOU'VE SEEN A GHOST.

YOU HAVE NO IDEA.

SHUT
LATER THAT NIGHT...
...BREE THOUGHT ABOUT CARRIE'S STORY IN THE PLAY. ABOUT GABRIELLE ASHFORD WHO ONCE PLAYED CARRIE. AND ABOUT WHAT SHE, BREE, SHOULD DO NEXT.
SHE FILLED HER MIND WITH ANYTHING AND EVERYTHING TO BLOCK OUT SEEING THAT HAUNTING FACE WHEN SHE CLOSED HER EYES.
MAYBE MEGAN'S RIGHT, SHE THOUGHT. THE PRESSURE OF BEING IN THE PLAY, THE WEIRD CONNECTIONS BETWEEN THE STORY AND MY REAL LIFE...
...THE LINES ARE BLURRING. I DON'T KNOW WHERE CARRIE ENDS AND I BEGIN.
AS BREE FINALLY DRIFTED OFF TO SLEEP, SHE CAME TO A DECISION.
SHE DIDN'T WANT TO DIG ANY FURTHER. SHE WOULD DO ANYTHING TO GET HER LIFE BACK TO NORMAL. EVEN IF IT MEANT QUITTING THE PLAY.

THE NEXT DAY...
...AT REHEARSAL...
PLACES, PEOPLE!
LOTS TO DO! WE OPEN IN TWO DAYS!
MS. HOLLOWS...?
YES, GABRIELLE-
I HAVE SOMETHING I NEED TO TALK TO YOU ABOUT.
AFTER WE RUN THE PHONE CALL SCENE. TAKE YOUR PLACE.

BREE COULDN'T EXPLAIN IT. SHE WAS IN A STATE OF PANIC A MOMENT AGO, BUT NOW...
...SOMETHING WAS DIFFERENT. ALMOST AS IF HER FEARS WERE MELTING AWAY.
WELL, WHAT ARE YOU WAITING FOR? PLACES!
C'MON, *CARRIE*! WE'VE GOT A SCENE TO DO.
BREE COULDN'T DISAPPOINT HER FRIENDS AND CLASSMATES. SHE COULDN'T UP AND QUIT THE PLAY.
IT WAS AS IF THIS STAGE WAS INFLUENCING HER, TELLING HER... *YOU CAN'T LEAVE*.
OKAY, PEOPLE! THE PHONE SCENE. I REALLY WANT TO BELIEVE THE FEAR.

BRRIIIIIIIING!
WHO IN THE WORLD COULD BE CALLING ME? IT'S SO LATE.
HELLO...?
LEAVE NOW... AND NEVER COME BACK...OR YOU'LL BE SORRY.
CLUNK!

THAT HAD TO BE A PRANK CALL, RIGHT? TELL ME IT WAS A PRANK CALL.
ONLY ONE WAY TO FIND OUT. I'M GOING TO CALL THE OPERATOR.
SPIIIN-CLICK-CLICK-CLICK-CLICK
THE NUMBER YOU HAVE DIALED IS NOT IN SERVICE. PLEASE CHECK THE NUMBER AND DIAL AGAIN.
BEEEEEP! EH-EH-EH-EH-EH
AAAAAAND SCENE! LET'S RUN IT AGAIN FROM THE TOP. RIGHT AWAY!
AND CAN WE MAKE SURE THE PHONE RING IS LOUDER? I WANT IT TO REALLY MAKE THE AUDIENCE JUMP.

A FEW HOURS LATER...
I CAN'T BELIEVE WE RAN THAT SAME SCENE FOUR TIMES IN A ROW. WAS IT ME?

NO! YOU'RE AMAZING! IT WAS A TECH THING WITH THE PHONE NOT BEING LOUD ENOUGH-

GASP!
BRRIIIIIIIING!

THAT SCARED ME! I THOUGHT YOU KEPT YOUR PHONE ON VIBRATE.
BRRIIIIIIIING!

I THOUGHT I DID TOO.
BRRIIIIIIIING!

Incoming call
UNKNOWN CALLER
BRRIIIIIIIING!
DECLINE
ANSWE

HELLO...?
LEAVE NOW AND NEVER COME BACK... OR YOU'LL BE SORRY... GABRIELLE.

CHAPTER 10
UNKNOWN CALLER
CALL ENDED
DON'T FREAK OUT—THIS HAS GOT TO BE SOME KIND OF PRANK, BREE. SOMEONE WHO WAS AT REHEARSAL AND SAW THE SCENE WE JUST DID.
SOMEONE WITH A VERY SICK SENSE OF HUMOR. SOMEONE WHO CALLS YOU "GABRIELLE."
TIFFANY.
C'MON, I DIDN'T SEE HER LEAVE YET. SHE'S GOTTA BE INSIDE.
I'M PUTTING A STOP TO THIS RIGHT NOW. I'VE HAD ENOUGH OF HER GAMES.

GASP!
KEUP

IF IT ISN'T THE BIG STAR OF THE PLAY. HERE TO CLAIM THE BIGGEST DRESSING ROOM, GABRIELLE?
WHY ARE YOU DRESSED LIKE THIS?
IT'S MY COSTUME. DUH. THEY TOLD ME TO STAY AFTER FOR A FINAL FITTING TODAY.
MAKEUP
WERE YOU AT MY HOUSE LAST NIGHT, DRESSED LIKE THIS?
HA! I WOULDN'T BE CAUGHT DEAD AT YOUR HOUSE.
DID YOU JUST CALL TO THREATEN ME?
WHAT ARE YOU TALKING ABOUT?
TELL ME YOU DIDN'T JUST CALL MY PHONE AND SAY WHAT CARRIE HEARS ON HER PHONE IN THE PLAY.
UM, OKAY, IF IT'LL GET YOU OUT OF MY FACE. I DIDN'T JUST CALL YOUR PHONE AND SAY—
I DON'T BELIEVE YOU!

YOU'VE BEEN MESSING WITH ME SINCE AUDITIONS!
YOU DON'T DESERVE THIS PART!
WHOA, CALM DOWN, TIME OUT! HOLD THE PHONE!
OH NO... IT'S HER AGAIN.
BRRIIIIIIIING!
BRRIIIIIIING!

BRRIIIIIING!
DON'T LOOK AT ME. MY PHONE IS IN MY LOCKER.

BRRIIIIIIIING!
Incoming call
UNKNOWN CALLER
DECLINE

TAP
HELLO...?

LEAVE NOW AND NEVER COME BACK, OR YOU'LL BE SORRY...
GABRIELLE.
WHO IS THIS?!!
HELLO????
CALL ENDED
OKAY, THAT WAS REALLY SCARY.
YEAH, "SCARY" HAS BEEN MY LIFE SINCE I STARTED THIS PLAY.
SORRY I ACCUSED YOU. I GOTTA GO.
BREE, WAIT UP!

BREE WALKED HOME, NOT KNOWING WHAT TO BELIEVE NOW.
SHE WAS SO SURE TIFFANY HAD BEEN TORMENTING HER. BUT IT WAS CLEAR SHE WAS NOT THE ONE MAKING THE CALLS.
BREE'S MIND FLASHED TO MEGAN. SHE KNEW HER SISTER DIDN'T WANT TO SHARE THE SPOTLIGHT.
BUT THERE WAS NO WAY IT WAS HER FACE BREE SAW WHEN THE LIGHTS WENT OUT LAST NIGHT. MEGAN HAD NEVER LEFT HER PARENTS' SIDE.

AND THEN THERE WAS THE MYSTERIOUS MS. HOLLOWS. THE ONLY PERSON AT SCHOOL WHO CALLED HER "GABRIELLE," OTHER THAN TIFFANY.
BREE NEVER GOT TO ASK HER WHY SHE DID THAT, OR IF MILLIE THE GHOST WAS NAMED AFTER MILDRED P. WORMHOUSE, OR IF THE PLAY ITSELF WAS REALLY CURSED.
ALL BREE KNEW FOR CERTAIN WAS THAT MS. HOLLOWS WANTED HER TO BE IN THE PLAY. WHICH MEANT SHE WOULDN'T BE THE ONE SCARING HER AWAY. ***RIGHT***?
***SO WHO IS IT,*** BREE WONDERED. ***WHO CALLED ME TO THREATEN ME? OR WAS IT A WARNING? AND SHOULD I LISTEN?***

SIGH
SO I'M RIGHT BACK WHERE I STARTED, SHE REALIZED.
STILL IN THE PLAY.
STILL WANTING TO QUIT THE PLAY.
STILL NOT GOING TO QUIT THE PLAY.

IT'S LIKE DEALING WITH TWO DIFFERENT VOICES ARGUING IN MY HEAD.
LIKE TWO BREES.
UGH, THIS PLAY IS TEARING ME APART!
SPLAAAAAASH

CHAPTER 11

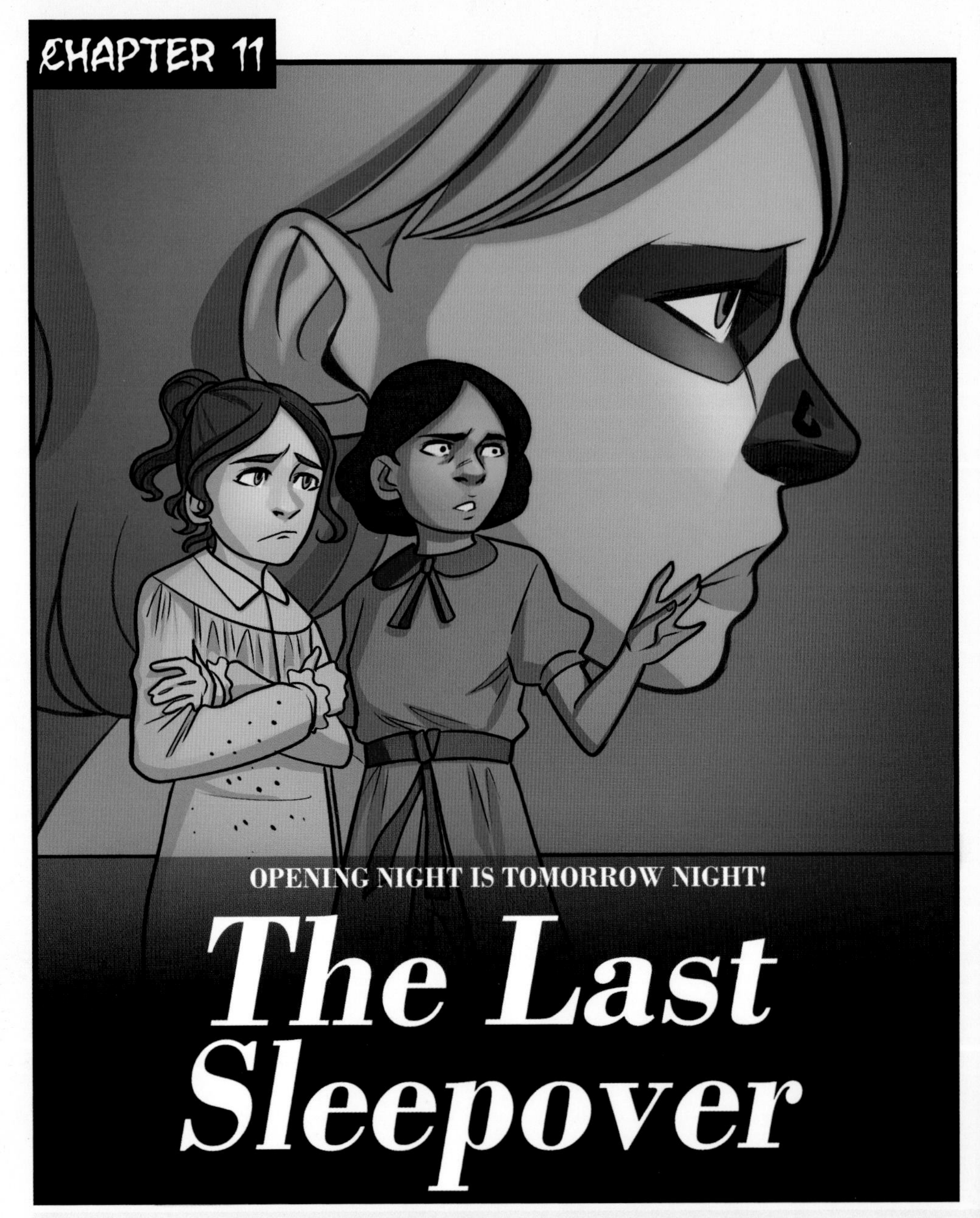


TICKETS STILL AVAILABLE AT DRAMA BOX OFFICE.
SEE MS. HOLLOWS FOR MORE INFORMATION.

**Written by Mildred P. Wormhouse**
**Directed by Ms. Hollows**

THE DAY BEFORE OPENING NIGHT...
FACE IT, BREE, YOU'RE NOT READY FOR THIS.
The Last Sleepover
Written by Mildred P. Wormhouse
Directed by Ms. Hollows
BUZZZZ
BUZZZ
BUZZZ
7:14 AM
MELISSA
Hey, need a ride to school? We're about to leave but can pick u up on the way.
TAP
TAP
TAP
TAP

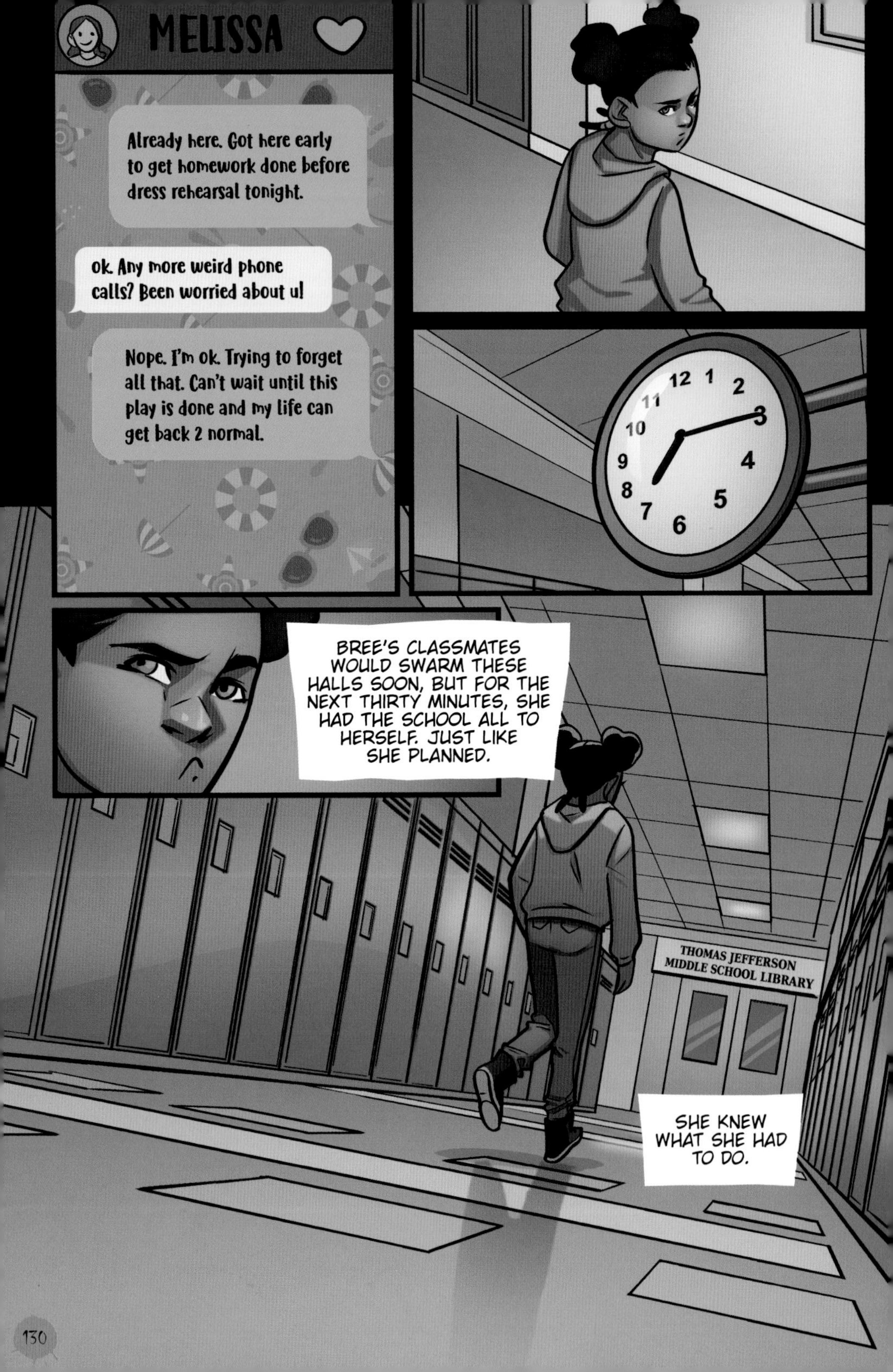
MELISSA
Already here. Got here early to get homework done before dress rehearsal tonight.
ok. Any more weird phone calls? Been worried about u!
Nope. I'm ok. Trying to forget all that. Can't wait until this play is done and my life can get back 2 normal.
BREE'S CLASSMATES WOULD SWARM THESE HALLS SOON, BUT FOR THE NEXT THIRTY MINUTES, SHE HAD THE SCHOOL ALL TO HERSELF. JUST LIKE SHE PLANNED.
THOMAS JEFFERSON MIDDLE SCHOOL LIBRARY
SHE KNEW WHAT SHE HAD TO DO.

SEARCH!!!
MILDRED P. WORM ...
TYPE
TYPE
TYPE
TYPE
...WORMHOUSE.
TYPE
TYPE
TYPE
MILDRED P. WORMHOUSE
All Images Videos More
http://playwright'scorner.com › mildredp.worm
MILDRED P. WORMHOUSE INTERVIEW — PLAYWRIGHT'S CORNER
Wormhouse revealed the tragic inspiration for her original play, The Last Sleepover.
'I was endlessly tormented by one particular bully,' she said.
MILDRED P. WORMHOUSE
All Images Videos More
CLICK
http://playwright'scorner.com › mildredp.worm
MILDRED P. WORMHOUSE INTERVIEW — PLAYWRIGHT'S CORNER
Wormhouse revealed the tragic inspiration for her original play, The Last Sleepover.
'I was endlessly tormented by one particular bully,' she said.

Wormhouse revealed the tragic inspiration for her original play, **THE LAST SLEEPOVER**. "I was endlessly tormented by one particular bully," she said.

"In my play, she's called Carrie. But I should have called her by the real girl's name—Gabrielle. Gabrielle turned everyone at school against me. She made my life miserable and made sure I never got invited to any sleepovers, never made any friends. She turned me into a ghost in my own life, so I gave the ghost my name, Millie. Short for Mildred. "

THIS WHOLE PLAY IS ABOUT REVENGE.

AND I'M THE TARGET!

SHUT
WHO'S THERE?!
BREE STARED INTO THE DARKNESS, HEARING ANOTHER NOISE...
...LIKE THE SOFT FOOTSTEPS OF SOMEONE RUNNING DOWN THE AISLE!
THUMP
THUMP
THUMP
SCIENCE
HELLO!
FWOOOOMMP!
I KNOW YOU'RE HERE! COME OUT!

BREE CAUGHT A GLIMPSE OF A SHADOW CHARGING OUT THROUGH THE DOORS–
*STOP!* PLEASE...
I NEED TO KNOW...WHAT'S GOING ON. SHOW YOURSELF.
BREE SAW THE FACE OF A GIRL. A GIRL ABOUT HER AGE.
BUT SHE COULDN'T PLACE HER.
WHAT ARE YOU DOING HERE? WHAT IS THIS ALL ABOUT?
THE GIRL SAID NOTHING. SHE SIMPLY TURNED AND RAN!

107D
CHASED AFTER HER. SHE WANTED ANSWERS.
SHE WANTED THEM BADLY ENOUGH TO CHASE A MYSTERIOUS STRANGER INTO THE DARK.
FLING!
SHE WAS GOING TO GET ANSWERS, AND SHE WAS GOING TO GET THEM NOW...
...SO THAT WHEN THE CURTAIN WENT UP TOMORROW NIGHT, ALL THIS CRAZINESS WOULD BE BEHIND HER.
BALCONY
The Last Sleepover

BALC
ONCE SHE REACHES THE BALCONY, THERE'S NOWHERE ELSE TO RUN, BREE THOUGHT AS HER FEET POUNDED THE STAIRS.
I'VE GOT HER NOW. AND SHE'LL TELL ME WHO SHE IS AND WHAT HAS BEEN GOING ON!
BALCONY

THERE'S NOWHERE ELSE TO GO.
YOU CAN'T RUN ANYMORE.
ARE YOU THE ONE WHO CALLED ME? WHO'S BEEN PLAYING TRICKS ON ME? TRYING TO SCARE ME INTO QUITTING THE PLAY?
WELL, IT ENDS HERE. I'M NOT SCARED OF YOU ANYMORE.
TURN AROUND SO I CAN SEE YOUR FACE.

AM I DREAMING THIS? AM I ASLEEP BACK AT HOME?
NO.
WHAT'S HAPPENING TO ME?
LEAVE NOW AND NEVER COME BACK...OR YOU'LL BE SORRY...
YOU'RE NOT A GHOST...YOU'RE ME? BUT *I'M* ME. HOW...?
THIS IS ALL TOO MUCH...
GABRIELLE, PLEASE–

BREE WAS SO STUNNED BY SEEING HER OWN FACE—HEARING HER OWN VOICE—THAT SHE DIDN'T FEEL HER FEET STUMBLING BACKWARDS TOWARD THE STAIRS...
SMACK-THWACK-THUMP
THUNK
UNNNHHH... HELP...SOMEONE... HELP...
THE LAST THING BREE REMEMBERED SEEING WAS HER OWN FACE LOOKING DOWN AT HER FROM THE TOP OF THE STAIRS.
SHE SWORE THE OTHER BREE WAS SMILING AT HER...
...AND THEN EVERYTHING WENT DARK.

# CHAPTER 12

BREE OPENED HER EYES SLOWLY.

AT FIRST, SHE COULD NOT MAKE SENSE OF HER SURROUNDINGS. SHE FELT HER HEAD RESTING ON A PILLOW.

HER BLURRY VISION BEGAN TO CLEAR AND SHE COULD MAKE OUT A CEILING LIGHT IN A WHITE ROOM–

YOU'RE IN THE HOSPITAL, SWEETHEART.
THAT WAS QUITE A FALL YOU TOOK, BUT THE DOC SAYS YOU'RE GOING TO BE JUST FINE.
NICE TO SEE YOU AWAKE.
I FELL...? IT WASN'T ALL A DREAM?

I WISH IT HAD BEEN A DREAM!
WHAT DAY IS IT? WHAT ABOUT THE PLAY?
HONEY, RELAX. YOU'VE BEEN ASLEEP A FEW DAYS.
THE PLAY WAS SUPPOSED TO OPEN YESTERDAY, BUT IT WAS POSTPONED AFTER YOUR FALL.

CAN'T STAGE A PLAY WITHOUT THE LEAD, RIGHT?

EVERYONE WAS JUST RELIEVED THE PLAY WAS POSTPONED. BECAUSE OF WHAT HAPPENED.

WHAT HAPPENED?

CLICK
GET WELL SOON
...AS YOU CAN SEE, CREWS ARE STILL SORTING THROUGH THE DAMAGE AT THOMAS JEFFERSON MIDDLE SCHOOL AFTER AN ACCIDENTAL GAS LEAK CAUSED A SMALL EXPLOSION AND FIRE IN THE AUDITORIUM...
...YESTERDAY AT SEVEN-THIRTY P.M....
...THE EXACT TIME THE SCHOOL PLAY WAS TO BEGIN. FORTUNATELY, THE AUDITORIUM WAS EMPTY AT THE TIME OF THE BLAST AND NO ONE WAS SERIOUSLY INJURED.
AN EXPLOSION? AT THE EXACT TIME I WOULD HAVE BEEN ON STAGE!
I MEAN, I COULD HAVE BEEN, I WAS ALMOST-
YOU WERE LUCKY. WE ALL WERE.

I'M NOT HAPPY YOU FELL, BUT BECAUSE YOU GOT HURT, NO ONE WAS ANYWHERE NEAR THAT BLAST.
YOU ACCIDENTALLY SAVED THE DAY. AND YOURSELF.
NO, NOT ME. THE OTHER ME. SHE WAS TRYING TO SAVE ME THE WHOLE TIME.
HUH?
CONCUSSION TALK. LET BREE GET SOME REST. SHE'S BEEN THROUGH A LOT.
TRY AND SLEEP NOW. WE'LL BE HERE WHEN YOU WAKE UP.
THE OTHER BREE...

BREE FELL INTO A DREAM...
BUT THIS DREAM WAS CALMING RATHER THAN ODD OR TERRIFYING.
IT'S YOU. I MEAN...
...IT'S *ME*, I GUESS.
COME. WALK WITH ME.
THE PLAY WAS CURSED. IT'S ALWAYS BEEN CURSED.
WHETHER BY EXPLOSION OR A LIGHT FALLING, WHOEVER PLAYS CARRIE IS DESTINED TO DIE. UNTIL NOW.
THANK YOU FOR SAVING ME. AND FOR SAVING ALL OF MY FRIENDS. OR SHOULD I THANK MYSELF?
IT'S COMPLICATED.

I'M YOU, OR RATHER, YOUR SPIRIT. I'M THE GHOST OF YOU WHO WOULD HAVE DIED IN THE EXPLOSION—IF YOU HADN'T TRIPPED AND FALLEN.

THERE ARE MANY TIME LINES THAT RUN PARALLEL TO ONE ANOTHER, BASED ON THE CHOICES WE MAKE A HUNDRED TIMES A DAY.

I MADE OUR TIME LINES INTERSECT. I FOUND A WAY TO PORTAL TO YOUR TIME LINE THROUGH YOUR DREAMS. AND I USED IT TO COMMUNICATE WITH YOU.

THAT'S WHY ALL THAT WEIRD STUFF KEPT HAPPENING.
YES. SIMPLY TALKING WAS IMPOSSIBLE. I HAD TO USE WHATEVER I COULD TO WARN YOU.
BECAUSE OF HOW TIME LINES WORK, I COULD ONLY DO THINGS THAT WERE PART OF THE PLAY, SINCE THAT'S WHERE OUR LIVES CROSSED OVER.
THAT'S WHY IT SEEMED LIKE THINGS IN THE PLAY WERE HAPPENING IN YOUR REAL LIFE.

NOW THAT YOU'RE SAFE, I CAN GO BACK TO MY OWN TIME LINE AND FINALLY REST IN PEACE.
BEFORE BREE COULD SAY ANYTHING ELSE, HER OTHER SELF FADED AWAY.
THE REST OF THE DREAM SOON FADED WITH HER, LEAVING BREE IN THE MOST RESTFUL SLEEP OF HER LIFE.
SHE THOUGHT OF ALL THE GOOD THAT HAD COME FROM THE PLAY. HOW IT HELPED HER BREAK OUT OF HER SHELL AND TAUGHT HER HOW TO STAND UP FOR HERSELF.
SHE KNEW SHE WOULD GO ON STAGE AGAIN. AND NEXT TIME, SHE WOULD DO IT IN A PLAY THAT WAS *NOT* CURSED.

A FEW WEEKS LATER...
LET ME BE THE FIRST TO WELCOME YOU BACK TO SCHOOL, BREE!
IT'S GOOD TO SEE YOU BACK TOO, MR. GOMEZ.
I HOPE YOU'LL CONSIDER TRYING OUT FOR THE PLAY AGAIN.
YOU KNOW WHAT THEY SAY... THE SHOW MUST GO ON.
AS LONG AS IT'S NOT *THIS* SHOW.
THE LAST SLEEPOVER
THUNK!
Eagles
THAT ALL OF THEM?
I THINK SO...
Eagles

MEANWHILE...
SOMEWHERE ELSE...
THE LAST SLEEPOVER
THE SHOW MUST GO ON...
THE SHOW MUST GO ON!
HAHAHAHAHA!
THE SHOW WILL GO ON!

PROLOGUE
IN THE DARKNESS OF A FREEZING WINTER NIGHT, WITHOUT A COAT...
...ALL SHE FELT WAS THE COLD.
SLAM
SHE WAS SO FOCUSED ON THE TINGLING IN HER HANDS, THE NUMBNESS...
...THAT SHE DIDN'T EVEN NOTICE HOW THE WET, HEAVY SNOW HAD BEEN PILING UP FOR DAYS AND DAYS.

...WHEN THERE WAS SO MUCH OF IT.

CRAAASHH

THE SPICY AROMA OF PEPPERMINT SURROUNDED HER, JUST AS THE SNOW DID. IT CAME FROM THE NECKLACE OF MINTS AROUND HER NECK.
THE SMELL COMFORTED HER IN THOSE FINAL MOMENTS. ALONG WITH A VOW: *I WILL NOT BE FORGOTTEN...I WILL NOT BE FORGOTTEN...I WILL NOT BE FORGOTTEN...*

CHAPTER 1
IT HAPPENED HERE!
A freak avalanche claimed the life of Mary Owens, a local girl, almost sixty years ago.
RIIIIIIING RIIIIIIING
RIIIIIIING
I GOT IT, I'M CLOSER—
I WAS GOING TO GET IT—
HELLO? GARCIA RESIDENCE.
KELLY, HONEY, I'M GLAD YOU'RE HOME!
WE JUST ARRIVED. I GOTTA GET READY FOR MY PARTY. LOTS TO DO.

NO VACANCY
KELS, LISTEN, ABOUT THAT. DADDY AND I ARE STUCK IN PHILADELPHIA RIGHT NOW.
THEY CANCELED ALL THE FLIGHTS OUT OF THE AIRPORT BECAUSE OF THE SNOW.
WHAT ARE YOU AND DADDY GOING TO DO?
WE THOUGHT ABOUT RENTING A CAR, BUT THE ROADS ARE A MESS RIGHT NOW.
THE ONLY SENSIBLE THING IS...
...FOR US TO SPEND THE NIGHT IN A MOTEL HERE AND DRIVE BACK TOMORROW.
I NEED YOU AND RYAN TO STAY PUT. NO GOING OUTSIDE. AND LOCK THE DOORS.

CHRISSIE WILL BE STAYING OVER WITH YOU AND RYAN TONIGHT.
A BABYSIT-TER?! YOU GOT US A BABYSIT-TER? C'MON, I'M TOO OLD FOR THAT.
I KNOW YOU'RE IN MIDDLE SCHOOL, BUT I'M NOT LEAVING YOU AND YOUR BROTHER ALONE OVERNIGHT. IT'S NOT SAFE WITH THIS SNOWSTORM.
WHO'S ALONE? PAIGE AND JUNE ARE SLEEPING OVER, REMEMBER?
KELS, THAT CAN'T HAPPEN TONIGHT. NOT WITHOUT ME AND YOUR DAD THERE. YOU KNOW THAT.
THAT'S NOT FAIR! IT'S MY BIRTHDAY!

NO, IT'S NOT!
WE'LL MOVE YOUR BIRTHDAY TO NEXT WEEKEND. BESIDES, YOUR REAL BIRTHDAY ISN'T UNTIL TUESDAY ANYWAY.
BUT, MOM!
NO BUTS! NOW, LET ME TALK TO YOUR BROTHER.
THINK FAST, NERD!
I'M NOT A NERD.
CATCH
HI, MOM, KELLY THREW THE PHONE AT ME AND CALLED ME A NERD...
UH-HUH... YUP...

I WILL DEFINITELY MAKE SURE TO TELL HER THAT.
CAN CHRISSIE ORDER US PIZZA...?
AWESOME!
'KAY. BYE, MOM! WE WILL! LOVE YOU! LOVE TO DAD, TOO!
HEY, KELS, GUESS WHAT?
MOM SAID YOU CAN'T CALL ME A NERD ANYMORE AND—
HEY, WHAT IS THAT PICTURE? IS THAT SOME-ONE YOU KNOW?
NO, IT'S SOME GIRL A LONG TIME AGO.
IT'S FROM ONE OF MOM'S ARTICLES. SCARY STUFF.
THIS GIRL WAS BURIED ALIVE BY AN AVALANCHE. SHE SUFFOCATED UNDER THE WEIGHT OF ALL THE SNOW. JUST LIKE THE SNOW OUTSIDE...

AND DON'T MISS

YOU'RE INVITED TO A

# CREEPOVER

THE GRAPHIC NOVEL

THERE'S SOMETHING OUT THERE!

BY P. J. NIGHT